MW00955893

SHANNON CAUSTIN

MOUNT NEVERREST

Illustrated by
Oscar Nahuel Runo

© 2021 Shannon Caustin. All rights reserved.

No part of this book may be reproduced, stored in a retrieval system, or transmitted by any means without the written permission of the author.

AuthorHouse™
1663 Liberty Drive
Bloomington, IN 47403
www.authorhouse.com
Phone: 833-262-8899

Because of the dynamic nature of the Internet, any web addresses or links contained in this book may have changed since publication and may no longer be valid. The views expressed in this work are solely those of the author and do not necessarily reflect the views of the publisher, and the publisher hereby disclaims any responsibility for them.

Any people depicted in stock imagery provided by Getty Images are models, and such images are being used for illustrative purposes only. Certain stock imagery © Getty Images.

This book is printed on acid-free paper.

ISBN: 978-1-6655-2299-1 (sc)
ISBN: 978-1-6655-2298-4 (hc)
ISBN: 978-1-6655-2300-4 (e)

Library of Congress Control Number: 2021907807

Print information available on the last page.

Published by AuthorHouse 04/21/2021

authorHOUSE

MOUNT
NEVERREST

Once upon a time, a lady named Mary had
all the laundry done in her House.

And a great banquet was had in celebration of the valiant Mary who conquered the demon of Mount Neverrest after warring for many years.

But then the children came home
from school covered in mud...

As the muddied children began to clean up, Mary was becoming increasingly aware of the most unsettling feeling.

Though the merriment of the celebration echoed through the great hall, joy, laughter, and jubilation could not be further from Mary's mind.

Terror-stricken, she froze as an all too familiar scent wafted under her nose.

"It can't be", she gasped, barely audible as though if she spoke any louder it would beckon this monstrous being into existence.

Yet, as her eyes scanned the banquet hall, she realized that she was not the only one who could sense the impending abomination that was steadily gaining power.

Soon, the victorious cacophony shrank to a weary din of dread.

Mary's stomach churned as she slowly turned. There, emanating from the pile of mud-caked clothing was the great foe that had only moments ago been naught but a memory.

Determined not to be shaken, Mary planted her feet firmly before the beast and mustered her courage. "Rise up women of this great country!" she called out. "Rise up men and take up arms! We shall no longer be overcome by such a foe! We will be victorious!

Come children and band together with us. For when we fight as one, there is no enemy we cannot vanquish!"

Everyone in that great city heard Mary's call to arms and their resolve was stirred within them.

Then, from the midst of the crowd a small voice was heard,
"But... how?"

The question, small and unassuming as it
might be, struck like a punch to the gut.

The voice continued, "You were our hero. You were the one who withstood what no person before ever had, and won."

"But now the same evil that we thought
had been conquered is returning.
If you can't defeat it, how will any of us be able to?"

Mary was shaken. She didn't know how to respond. After all, what more could be done that she hadn't already tried?

As Mary scanned the crowd for the source
of these doubt filled queries, her eyes
met those of her daughter, Jenna.

"If you can't do it, mom, who can?" was her final plea.

The words hung in the air like a London fog,
heavy and oppressive. Then she turned her eyes
downcast as the ember of hope slowly dimmed.

A moment later, a strong hand rested on Jenna's shoulder.
"Take courage little one" a warm voice assured
as he lifted her face to meet his eyes.

Through her welling tears, she recognized her father's face, though she already knew by the sound of his voice it could be no one else.

She met his gaze with a weary grin.
"Your mother is very heroic indeed," he continued.

"We are all awestruck by what she has accomplished on her own. Such a defeat has never before been known among these peoples."

"But, it takes more than one hero standing alone to achieve true greatness. If we stand together as one city, one community, one family, there is no victory we cannot attain."

One by one, each of the citizens began to shout. "He's right!" called one "We can do this!" cried another "We can do it together!" shouted one more.

Their cheers renewed the resolve of each and every heart in the crowd, including Jenna's. And they all began hatching a plan that was sure to work.

One person suggested they build cages
to contain the dirty clothes.

Another suggested that they take turns
keeping watch over the growing Pile.

As soon as a cage was full, another group would take the clothes to be washed, dried and sorted.

Once all the laundry was clean, and separated, each member of the community would be sure to put their laundry in the proper place.

"What a brilliant plan!" Mary shouted. "But remember, in order for this to work, we must be vigilant. The moment any one of us lets down our guard, the entire chain is broken and the beast will regain power until it is beyond our control."

And with that, they sallied forth and tamed the mighty beast and the demon of Mount Neverrest was vanquished, not once and for all...

...but every single day.

The end